MONSTERS

W9-AUD-597

RUSSELL HOBAN

Illustrated by Quentin Blake

SCHOLASTIC HARDCOVER
SCHOLASTIC INC. / New York

Text copyright © 1989 by Russell Hoban.
Illustrations copyright © 1989 by Quentin Blake.
All rights reserved. Published by Scholastic Inc.
by arrangement with Victor Gollancz Ltd.
SCHOLASTIC HARDCOVER is a registered trademark
of Scholastic Inc.

No part of this publication may be reproduced in whole or in part, or stored
in a retrieval system, or transmitted in any form or by any means,
electronic, mechanical, photocopying, recording, or otherwise, without
written permission of the publisher. For information regarding permission,
write to Scholastic Inc., 730 Broadway, New York, NY 10003.

Library of Congress Cataloging in Publication Data
Hoban, Russell.
Monsters/Russell Hoban; illustrated by Quentin Blake.
p. cm.
Summary: John's obsession with drawing monsters takes him to a doctor,
where a startling discovery is made about the degree of reality of
John's drawings.
ISBN 0-590-43422-5
[1. Drawing—Fiction. 2. Monsters—Fiction.] I. Blake, Quentin.
ill. II. Title.
PZ7.H637Mp 1990
[E]—dc20
89-10628
CIP
AC
12 11 10 9 8 7 6 5 4 3 2 1   0 1 2 3 4 5/9
Printed in Hong Kong
First Scholastic printing, September 1990

John liked to draw monsters.

He drew monsters that looked like puddings
with teeth, he drew monsters that had hundreds
of eyes and odd numbers of ears, he drew scaly
monsters, furry monsters, vegetable and
mineral monsters, and unheard-of monsters that
were so monstrous they had to be invisible so
they wouldn't scare themselves to death.

He drew red, yellow, blue, green, and purple
monsters and he drew spotted monsters
and monsters that were all blotchy with
different colors.

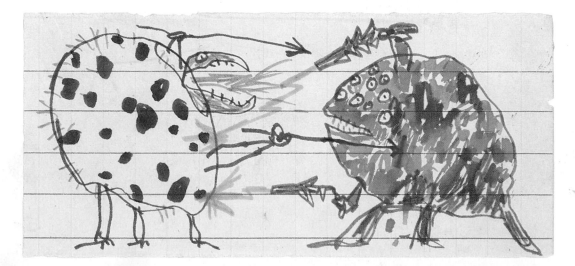

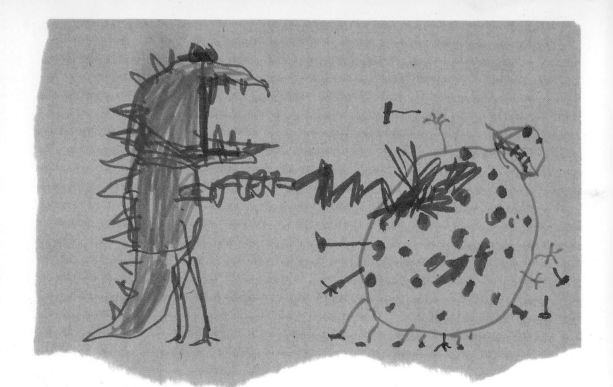

All of John's monsters were violent. They fought with passing strangers and random spacecraft and they fought with one another, and if they found themselves alone they made threatening noises to themselves while waiting for somebody ugly to turn up.

"*GNGGHHHH!*" they said, "*NNARRRGH!*" and "*XURRRVVV!*"

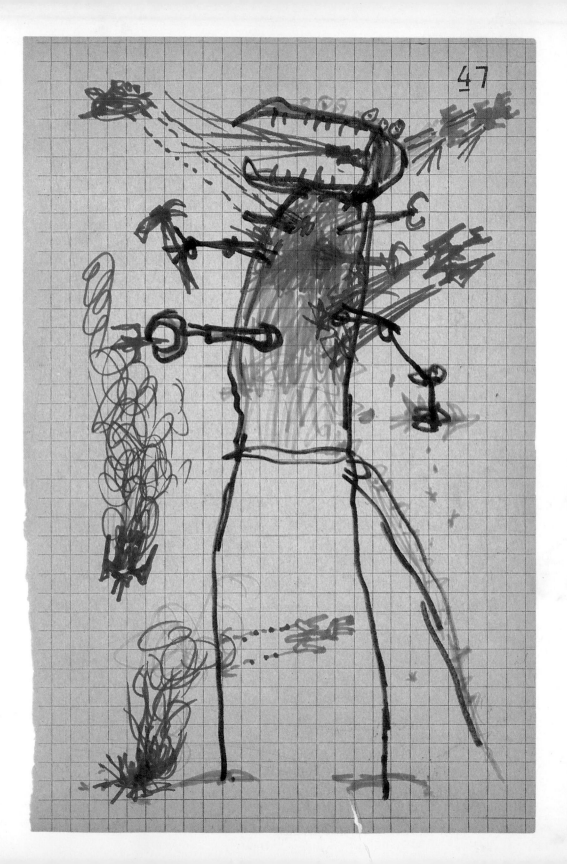
47

John's monsters breathed smoke and fire and they used their teeth and their claws when they fought.

They also used guided missiles, lasers,
bows and arrows, spears, clubs, and rocks.

John was drawing a battle between an army
of red monsters wielding hammers and an
army of green monsters with tongs when his mother
looked over his shoulder. "Don't you ever get tired
of drawing monsters?" she said.

"Not really," said John. "Monsters are my favorite thing to draw."

"Still," said Mom, "there are so many other nice things to draw. There are houses and trees and birds and animals."

"Monsters are animals," said John.

"I mean real animals like dogs and cats," said Mom, "or even lions and tigers if you like."

"Monsters are real," said John.

"Have you ever seen one?" said Mom.

"I've seen them on TV," said John.

"Yes," said Mom, "but have you ever seen one just walking around?"

"Not yet," said John.

"Everything all right at school?" said Dad.
"Getting on with the other boys and all that?"

"Yes," said John.

"And your teachers," said Mom, "what
about them?"

"They're all right," said John.

"Any trouble with any of your subjects?"
said Dad. "I used to have a terrible time with
math and history."

"I'm not having any trouble with anything,"
said John. "Have you got any really big
pieces of paper?"

"I've got some big sheets of brown wrapping paper," said Mom. She gave them to John.

"Thank you," said John. He took the wrapping paper and his felt-tip pens up to his room.

When Mom and Dad came up to kiss John
goodnight they saw that he'd done a drawing that
filled up a whole sheet of wrapping paper.

"What is it?" said Dad.

"It's the tip of a tail," said John.

"Very spiky," said Mom. "Where's the rest of
whatever it is?"

"Coming," said John.

"Must be pretty big," said Dad.

"I guess so," said John.

"What will it be?" said Mom.

"I don't know," said John. "I haven't seen the
other end of it yet."

When John was asleep Dad said to Mom, "That
drawing doesn't seem quite the same as John's
other drawings."

"No," said Mom, "it doesn't. It seems somehow
more *serious* than the others."

"It does," said Dad, "and if just the tip of the
tail filled up that big piece of paper the whole
thing must be very serious indeed."

The next day Mom and Dad went to see John's art teacher, Mr. Splodge. "What do you think of John's drawings?" said Dad.

"First-rate," said Mr. Splodge. "His monsters are in a class by themselves."

Mom showed him the drawing on the brown paper. "What do you think of this one?" she said.

"This tail is very well done," said Mr. Splodge. "It almost jumps right off the paper at you, doesn't it."

"John says the rest of it is coming," said Dad.

"Should be quite impressive," said Mr. Splodge.

"You're not bothered about it?" said Mom.

"Why should I be bothered?" said Mr. Splodge.

"Well, it's such a serious-looking tail," said Dad, "and whatever's on the other end of it is going to be so very big."

"I shouldn't worry about it if I were you," said Mr. Splodge. "Boys are naturally a little monstrous."

The next morning Mom and Dad found another drawing on John's desk. "I think we ought to talk to Dr. Plunger," said Dad. So they went to Dr. Plunger's office and showed him the two drawings.

"This could be something very big," said Dr. Plunger.

"That's what we thought," said Mom.

"Are you worried about it?" said Dr. Plunger.

"Yes, we are," said Dad.

Dr. Plunger wrote out a prescription. "Take the
tablets as directed," he said, "and if the drawings
continue let me see the next one."

The next day Mom and Dad brought in a third
drawing.

"Dear me," said Dr. Plunger. "Perhaps I'd
better have a chat with John."

When Mom and Dad brought John in for a chat, Dr. Plunger said, "Tell me about these drawings, John."

"I haven't got one piece of paper that's big enough," said John. "That's why I have to do it this way."

"Looks like it's going to be something really big," said Dr. Plunger.

"I can't say till I've seen the whole thing," said John.

"If I give you some felt-tip pens and some brown wrapping paper," said Dr. Plunger, "do you think you could finish it for me?"

"Are you sure you want me to?" said John.

"Yes, indeed," said Dr. Plunger.

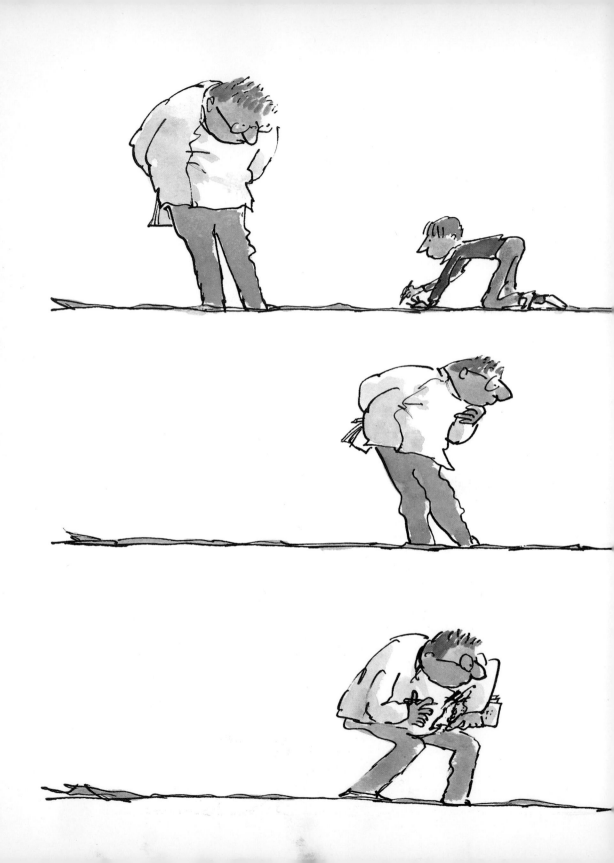

"All right," said John. When Dr. Plunger gave him
the paper and the pens he began to draw very fast,
moving from one sheet of brown paper to the next.

In the waiting room Mom and Dad heard a noise like two or three heavy metal rock bands all playing at once. There wasn't a lot of music to it, it was mostly thumping and bumping and crashing around. After a while it stopped and they heard John say, "See you," then he came out of Dr. Plunger's office with a big smile on his face.

"Quite a lively time you seemed to be having in there," said Dad.

"You look very relaxed," said Mom.

"I feel pretty good, actually," said John.

"Did I hear you say you'd be seeing him again?" said Mom.

"Who?" said John.

"Dr. Plunger," said Mom.

"I don't think so," said John.

"Get everything worked out, did you?" said Dad.

"Oh yes," said John, "everything worked out."

"No more monster drawings?" said Mom.

"Drawings?" said John as the door behind him slowly opened, "Who needs drawings?"

#4912
4/91
$10.27

The End